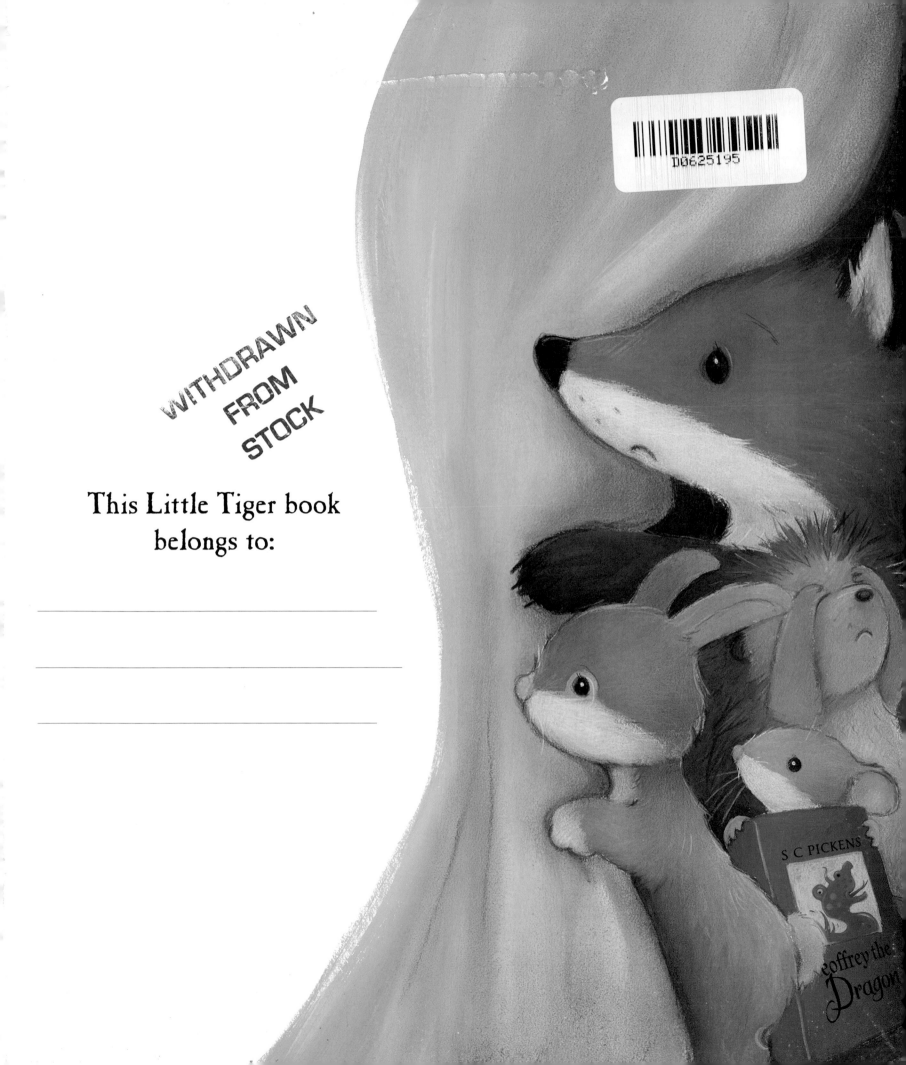

This Little Tiger book
belongs to:

_____

_____

_____

S C PICKENS

eoffrey the
Dragon

For Dad x
~ P B

For Amanda, Hilary, Lydia, Mary, Thérèse, Vanessa
and Yvo who would love Bear's house of books!
~ A E

LITTLE TIGER PRESS LTD,
an imprint of the Little Tiger Group,
1 The Coda Centre, 189 Munster Road,
London SW6 6AW
www.littletiger.co.uk

First published in Great Britain 2017
This edition published 2017

Text by Poppy Bishop
Text copyright © Little Tiger Press 2017
Illustrations copyright © Alison Edgson 2017

Alison Edgson has asserted her right to be identified as the illustrator
of this work under the Copyright, Designs and Patents Act, 1988

A CIP catalogue record for this book is available from the British Library

Printed in China · LTP/1400/1804/0417

2 4 6 8 10 9 7 5 3 1

BEAR's House of Books

Poppy Bishop

Alison Edgson

LITTLE TIGER
LONDON

Once, there lived four friends who loved stories. Every night, at bedtime, they read the same battered storybook. The cover was scuffed and the pages were sticky, but they didn't mind one bit. It had been theirs since they were all very little.

"Wouldn't it be nice," said Mouse one day at breakfast, "to read a new book?"

"A new book?" cried Fox. "But where would we get one?"

"Maybe you dig them up like potatoes," said Hedgehog hopefully.

"I know!" cried Rabbit.
"They fall from the sky like shooting stars!"

"Let's go on a book hunt and find out," said Mouse.

So they packed jam sandwiches and set off through the woods.

The friends searched the woods high and low.

"This is silly," grumbled Fox after a while. "You can't just *find* books."

"Then what's that?" said Hedgehog, pointing at something red under a bush. It had thick pages, a big, black title and smelt exactly like . . .

"A BOOK!" cheered Mouse. "It's a book!"

And what a fantastic story it was –
with a fire-breathing dragon for Rabbit,
and a good happy ending for Hedgehog.
"That was magical," Hedgehog sighed.
"It's my new favourite story,"
declared Fox.

But Mouse had spotted something
written inside.

This book belongs to:
Bear
The Twisted Oak
Thorny Lane
The Other Side of the Woods

KEEP YOUR PAWS OFF!

"Goodness!" said Hedgehog. "We had better return the book at once."

"Can't we keep it a little longer?" asked Rabbit.

But the friends knew deep down that they couldn't.

This book belongs to:
Bear
The Twisted Oak
Thorny Lane
the other side of the woods

KEEP YOUR PAWS OFF!

It was a long, hot trudge to Bear's house.
When they got there, no one answered Rabbit's
loud RAT-A-TAT-TAT on the door – and the
book wouldn't fit through the letterbox.

"Now what will we do?" huffed Fox.

"Look! An open window!" squeaked Mouse.

The friends lifted up the heavy book and pushed it through the window.

But Mouse forgot to let go
and fell in after it!

BUMP!
BUMP!
WHUMP!

"Ouch!" cried Mouse, landing
on a huge pile of . . .

. . . books! They were everywhere! Thin books,
chunky books. Funny books, sad books.
Whole, new worlds to hold in her hands.

"Look!" Mouse beamed as she let her friends in.

"Wow!" gasped Rabbit. "So many adventures!"

"And happy endings!" hurrahed Hedgehog.

"Let's get reading at once," said Fox.

Many wonderful stories later, the friends heard a **THUMP!**

"What's that?" gasped Fox.

It was getting closer . . . **THUMP! THUMP!**

And louder! **THUMP! THUMP! THUMP!**

"Someone's coming!" hissed Rabbit.

"Oh dear! We've been very naughty!" cried Hedgehog.

"This isn't our house and these aren't our books!"

"Quick," whispered Mouse.
"Hide!"

Bear clomped into the room.
He sat down with a HUFF
and reached for a book.

"Who's left sticky pawprints on this cover?" he grumbled. "And a **WHOLE** jam sandwich in the middle!" he rumbled.

"WHO'S BEEN READING MY BOOKS?!"

"We have," quavered four little voices.

"Scallywags!" bellowed Bear, whipping back the curtain.

"How dare you touch my books!"

"We're very sorry," squeaked Mouse.

"We found this book in the woods and—"

"That's mine!" cried Bear.

"It's my favourite!"

"It's our favourite too," said Rabbit.

"I liked the end," Hedgehog whispered. "I love happy endings."

"HMMPH!" grumped Bear. "I like happy endings too."

The four friends trooped towards the door.

"We really are sorry," called Mouse.

"We only have one book at home, you see."

"Wait," frowned Bear. "Only one book?"

He thought for a moment, and then picked
a storybook from the shelves. "If you wash
your sticky paws, you can stay and read
with me."

So Bear and the friends piled into an
armchair and read the story together.
They had so much fun, they
read another, and another,
until it was time to
go home.

"Can we come again?" asked Rabbit.
    "Hmmph!" said Bear. Then he smiled.
"I'd like that very much."

So the next day the friends all came back.

They even read Bear their own battered storybook.

And that gave Bear a very good idea . . .

Because books are wonderful to read alone,

but even better when shared.

MORE animal ADVENTURES from Little Tiger Press!

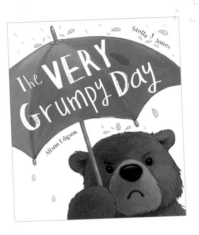

For information regarding any of the above titles
or for our catalogue, please contact us:

Little Tiger Press,
1 The Coda Centre,
189 Munster Road,
London SW6 6AW
Tel: 020 7385 6333
E-mail: contact@littletiger.co.uk
www.littletiger.co.uk